OTHER BOOKS BY KRISTIN ZAMBUCKA

Princess Ka'iulani of Hawai'i
(The Monarchy's Last Hope)

Kalākaua: Hawai'i's Last King

The High Chiefess Ruth Ke'elikōlani

Ano 'Ano: The Seed
The Mana Keepers
The Fire Lily

Kaumuali'i: King of Kaua'i

ANO 'ANO
THE SEED

The Classic Trilogy

Including
THE MANA KEEPERS
AND
THE FIRE LILY

KRISTIN ZAMBUCKA

MUTUAL PUBLISHING

ISBN 1-56647-709-3

Library of Congress Catalog Card Number:
2005920379

Cover Design by
Sachi Kuwahara Goodwin

First Printing, March 2005
1 2 3 4 5 6 7 8 9

Mutual Publishing, LLC
1215 Center Street, Suite 210
Honolulu, Hawai'i 96816
Ph: 808-732-1709 / Fax: 808-734-4094
email: mutual@mutualpublishing.com
www.mutualpublishing.com

Printed in Australia

INTRODUCTION

Mana is the life force itself emanating from a great universal source.

This sense of a higher power flowing through all living things; a force which could be harnessed by Man for his own use, was the basic concept underlying all thought in preChristian Polynesia. Dr. William Tufts Brigham, the first director of Honolulu's Bishop Museum, spent over forty years studying the kahuna of Hawaii with their astonishing ability to "harness the forces of nature and perform miracles." The Hawaiians had an effective prayer formula that consisted of planting a seed of thought and nourishing it daily with a gift of mana.

When the first company of Christian missionaries began preaching in Hawaii in 1820, they wielded a book magnificent in its content, but greatly misunderstood and misinterpreted. The well-meaning visitors translated its passages literally to the Islanders overlooking all of its truths veiled in symbolism and allegory.

A long period of painful confusion followed for the Hawaiian people. They were described as "heathens" for practicing their ancient rites, termed "immoral" for their liberal and healthy attitude towards sex and the life force and finally, during the 1890s, were forbidden to perform their "lewd and lascivious" hula (dance) which the Hawaiians themselves considered "an extension of the soul."

The visitors were ignorant of the teachings of the kahuna, of their multifaceted descriptions of human morality and their instructions regarding the subtle differences involved in what they considered the greatest sin of all... the sin of hurting another. The saddest feature of this conflict between the Hawaiians and the missionaries was that the Bible contained so many glimpses of similar teachings to what the Hawaiians had long been taught by their "Keepers of the Secret," the kahuna. Only the limited minds of the missionary interpreters got in the way of the merging of two enlightening paths to the one truth.

Sowing and reaping had long been a code for the Hawaiians. Of the many symbols used by the kahuna to veil their teachings, such as the "tree of life" and the "vine," the "seed" was the one most widely used.

So the Hawaiians took the Christian God, and gradually during the last 158 years, their beliefs came "full circle."

The mysteries of life were the same then as they are now... and human pain still seems without purpose, but insight provides hope. Although the kahuna trained in the old way have long since disappeared, the kahuna of today frequently use the Bible to solve human problems. All humanity is looking in the same direction, after all... but some are born to follow different paths.

After numerous years of research and painting throughout the Pacific area, I offer this volume as my own tribute, firstly to the Hawaiians whose images I borrowed to illustrate this book, and secondly to mankind's endless quest for a meaning to our existence.

Kristin Zambucka

ANO ANO: THE SEED

Ageless coconut palms guarded the seekers'
tryst against a backdrop of dark lofty
mountains, scanned by a golden sickle of moon
silently gleaming…

Androgynous in the shadows, they waited
without faces or names, cooled by the scented
leaves that brushed against them.

Three of the older ones rested with their bodies
stretched out face down so they could smell the
damp earth.

Like sphinxes their backs arched as they raised
their heads taking the weight on their
outstretched forearms.

In the moonlight they became dignified effigies
in stone… monuments to their old selves.

Their aura grew tense and vulnerable as they
inhaled the fragrant night… and examined their
feelings.

At last the stage was set for truth.

Long had they searched and far, in seemingly
endless circles outside themselves, for a
meaning to their existence.

The time had come for answers as their journey
took a new turn… inward.

"And what of life? Why are we here at all?" they asked.

And the old ones answered, too simply, that life is a series of lessons to be learned.

"But why all the suffering that haunts us throughout our years?" they questioned.

"We didn't ask to be born. Why must we pay such a price for this consciousness?"

"You were never born," they were told. "You can never die, so you were never born. Know that you ARE. Life is an endless chain of experiences as we grow spiritually back towards our source. Take charge of your consciousness.

Sowing and reaping is all you need to practice.

Plant well your good seeds and pluck up the bad."

"We are all on a spiral path.

No growth takes place in a straight line.

There will be setbacks along the way…

There will be shadows, but they will be balanced by patches of light and fountains of joy as we grow and progress.

Awareness of the pattern is all you need to sustain you along the way…"

"We all live many lives.

Even during our present span of days and nights… we may act out many roles.

We have all been all things, so never condemn another for what he may be.

Our circumstances may change… problems are presented… and complexes long buried may rise to the surface of the mind.

Some are hangovers from an endless past of struggles for survival."

"Know that there is a path to a higher consciousness within ourselves… and you alone are the keeper of that path… a path that can be blocked by the events of life.

Make amends for the wrong you have done to others and rid yourselves of guilt.

Free yourselves from injustice… and injustice will no longer stalk you.

Your suffering is only caused by your thoughts.

You are in charge of your mind… free it.

No difficulty has any power over you unless you give it that power.

Let past events fade away and don't allow them to paint dark colors on your future."

4

"And when the paralyzing ache of despair engulfs you, and you reel shaken from the blows that life deals you, and you scream out, demanding to know what you've done to deserve it…

And when you know that you can't take any more but it strikes you again, harder this time, from another side, and you are just hanging on by a thread until you feel yourself curl inward and die a little…

Know that there is a reason for it all…"

The old ones went on to explain the meaning of life itself… and they gave the listeners hope.

"We are not here for nothing," they said. "Life is not just a bad joke. Suffering unlocks the door to many answers and fire purifies. If you look back and examine some pain of the past, you will see that it taught you so much that no other teacher could…

Only when wounded do we stand still and listen.

Bleeding, you will be brought to your knees many times.

But somehow, nourished by an indomitable thread of strength within… you will go on.

Your eyes will not really see until they are incapable of tears.

Only when you can cry no more will you begin to grow."

"It is then that you will hear a voice within yourself.

It was there all the time, but you never listened before,

Faintly it will speak to you at first, but it will gradually grow louder and clearer the more you take heed of its message until one day it thunders inside you and you will have come home."

And listening… listening, they came to rely on its judgment.

They made fewer mistakes, as closing their eyes, ignoring appearances, they "saw" with that voice within and learned to trust it, as it was the nearest they came to hearing the voice of God.

Spirit alone is immortal.

Man is made up of ideas… and ideas will guide his life.

The physical body is lent to us so that spirit may come into contact with matter.

Neither worship that body nor neglect it… but respect the instrument you have been given to pursue this earthly life.

We are all children of one father.

The same essence of life dwells in all of us...
to protect and nourish; to heal and to guide.

If we turn to it and trust it, we will not be
turned away.

Once you find this presence you will rest
secure.

You can then be a father to someone else.

The presence within is the true father of man.

And all that the father has is already yours...

For you and the father are one...

Children do not remain children forever, but
move through various stages toward maturity.

And so it is with consciousness.

We outgrow people, places and things as we
unfold.

We shed the old self to make way for the new
self to be born.

There is no death, but a constant cycle of
rebirth...

An endless chain as we grow towards spiritual
perfection.

And for long hours they recited flowery words of praise to this benevolent friend they had found… this ancient patriarch with the long white beard and the powers of a magician who would dissolve their troubles with a wave of his hand and set things right for them.

But still their prayers went unheard… and they lamented the deaf ears of God who heard them not.

And seeing their dilemma the old ones described for the listeners the most sacred truth of all…

The very nature of the presence they must call God… and for some strange reason, describe as a man.

"Eradicate all thoughts about the appearance of this being," they said, "for you can never know God with your mind.

Cease thinking of God and begin sensing and feeling his oneness with yourself… then he will exist.

Never was God outside yourself or separate from you.

We need only be receptive and the substance of his power will flow through us.

We are really but instruments and we will be used.

It is only through our consciousness that God can enter this world.

He then translates into our human experience.

The blessing will manifest in the form of material advantages... a bearing of fruit."

And the night was still as they were given the greatest gift that mankind can receive... the formula for having their prayers answered.

But there was one essential condition to observe:

Would the prayer hurt someone else?

For the only real "sin" to them was in hurting another's feelings or coveting his material possessions.

HO'ANO

Making The Seed

Form a clear unwavering picture in your mind... of the condition or object you desire.

Be very careful of the details of your picture for the subconscious mind that will receive it is sharply accurate... and you will get the exact replica of what you envisage.

Forget the old condition entirely... let it fall away from your mind.

Clearly see the new desired state.

Paint the picture carefully inside your head…
and resist any changing of your mind.

Act then as if you had already received the
condition for which you ask.

Feel it already upon you with the love or joy or
whatever emotion you would experience if it
were so.

Act it out.

For this subconscious mind of which we
speak… this unihipili… is like a child.

It loves pictures and will respond also to any
emotional surge you project to it.

Daily thereafter gather mana by taking four
deep breaths and offer it as a gift to the God
within you.

Then after this offering each day, recall the
"seed picture" of your desire and offer it anew
also… to the same higher consciousness within
yourself.

This practice will strengthen the picture and
make it clearer as it nears the stage where it
will take form.

Until your seed bears its fruit… hold it close to
you as a secret… for any mention of its
contents to another will spill its power to reach
fruition.

Wash out all your doubts… they can so
discourage the subconscious that the daily rite

will be interrupted and your fruit will "wither
on the vine."

And the truth of it shook them as they
wandered awestruck in the shadow of the
mountain -
WE CREATE GOD.

And the voice inside them thundered:
IF YOU BELIEVE IN ME… I AM.

The impact of their discovery was too great and
too simple to believe at first.

How could the object of their long quest be so
close at hand?

And they doubted and were distressed at the
deceit of the voice they were learning to trust.

And the old ones saw their confusion and
instructed them to accept the presence within
and to nourish it with words and thoughts and
offerings of mana.

So they talked to this presence that dwelt
within.

And they knew at last the peace of answered
prayers.

And the hand of the father rested on them.

"Do not condemn your days," the old ones said.

"Stop the battle within and strive to understand
yourself instead.

Live well this life… plant good seeds… find the presence of God within and seek its help."

The next life and the life before this one were of little interest to the people of old.

But the more they pondered the seeming futility of this incarnation with all its pain and disappointment… they were prompted to ask:

"And what of former lives?"

And the old ones answered:

"There is no real remembrance. A memory here… a vision there… but you will not know who you once were or whom you may yet become."

And they were taught the laws of life… that their treatment of others would return at last upon themselves.

Those who cheat will be cheated.

Those who slander will be slandered.

For every lie you tell… you will be lied to.

Brutality will meet with brutality.

We get what we give and to the same degree.

And not always from the same people with whom we've dealt.

But somewhere… sometime … someone will treat you in like manner.

The good that we do to others will return also.

For your kindness to strangers you will receive hospitality in far places yourself.

Understand the troubles of others who come to you with their souls bared... and when you cry yourself, you will be sympathetically understood.

We get what we give.

Like always attracts like.

This is the law and it is inevitable.

We cannot escape the results of our actions.

Security takes root only in your state of mind.

Why seek the approval of others?

You tried to make them like you, but the feeling of comfort you sought did not come.

And the old ones understood...

"You will find no security in acting that way," they said.

"Anxiety will soon cramp you again like the chill of dawn, and you will have forfeited your integrity."

We outgrow people, places, and things as we unfold.

We may be saddened when old friends say their piece and leave our lives... but let them go.

They were at a different stage... looking in a different direction.

They stood still while you advanced in your thoughts and aspirations and the friendship was strained for a long time, but neither party had the heart to let it go.

Remember we have no duty to drag them along with us as we grow.

There is nothing to give each other any more... and one day you see a stranger behind the other's eyes-eyes you once thought you knew.

Each life has its own special design.

We only acquire and keep what truly belongs to us.

There is trouble if we try to take what is not ours or what is not right for our development.

Sometimes we are violently pitchforked away from someone or something that we have wanted.

And we rage against the stroke of fate that breaks up the alliance.

But it may have been disastrous had we stayed.

If we look back at the remade situation, all evens out and harmony is restored in the end.

We find our right place at the right time and with the right person.

And if your spirit does not rest easily inside

you, if you yearn for another form, it may be a hangover from a former life... a shadow of someone you once were.

We bring strange yearnings with us on our journey from the past, for somewhere along the line, we have been all things... man and woman... beggar and merchant... pauper and potentate.

Though mankind is only one, it wears a million masks.

There is a secret life in nature where both male and female can exist in the same plant... and have we not been told that Man's earthly predecessor was an androgyne?

For mana is the silent force permeating all of nature... the magnificent energy flowing through all living things.

It can be harnessed and gathered by man to increase his own power... if only he can find its source.

All living matter is modeled by it.

And we spend our whole lives seeking it as a holy quest... and our hearts will find no peace until they rest in it, for it flows from the supreme being we call God.

Once found, the whole world takes on a new splendor.

It becomes a thing of mysterious and sacred significance.

The seed of all things lies buried within us until the gift of mana is offered to it.

A seed regenerates and never dies.

It sprouts and grows again…and life continues in a never ending cycle.

All our strength and power lie in finding our source of mana.

If we truly find it and recognize its source, it will never cease to flow.

It is an endless channel of blessings.

Pain accompanies all birth.

There is pain when we are born and there is pain when we are re-born as old facets of the personality die away… or are brutally torn out of our life pattern… to make way for the new.

In breaking down the old future, one's world may seem to fall apart.

Trouble will enter the life like a storm…

A tempest will rage.

Do not resist… there is a balancing power at work… for your new self is about to enter the world.

Though you may travel far you will meet only what you carry with you, for every man is a mirror.

We see only ourselves reflected in those around us.

Their attitudes and actions are reflections of our own.

The whole world and its conditions has its counterpart within us all.

Turn the gaze inward... correct yourself and your world will change.

Forgive yourself for past mistakes.

Let them go from your mind... the only place they ever were... hanging on like gnawing aches that spoil your present experience of life.

Stop imposing the agony of remorse on yourself, and see yourself acting back then as a child... without insight... without maturity.

You have grown since.

Your mistakes contributed to that growth.

You would not act the same way now.

You cannot change the past... but you can change your thoughts about it.

An attitude is ours to control.

We are the creators.

Change your thoughts and you change your

world.

Life is full of change.

The good passes... but so does the bad.

Nothing remains the same in this unstable world.

Not a single element of anything... physical or mental... is the same today as it was yesterday.

When we are down at the bottom of the pit of despair... the only way to go is up.

If we only wait a little... the cycle, the endless unfailing tide of things will sweep us up again.

"Without darkness," said the old ones, "we would not appreciate the light when it comes."

What then do we owe to others?

And they were told that we owe them nothing except to grow mature ourselves... to find the real self within us all.

You cannot help anyone... but you can be the friend that they always hoped existed.

BE something for them.

Out of their own confusion others may try to dictate our duties to us.

Drop such burdens.

We cannot love those we feel it our duty to love.

Face the reality of the person's makeup.

We owe him nothing if his personality repels our love or kindness.

We must all earn the right to be loved.

And do not expect love if you are incapable of giving it.

Long will you wander in a wilderness of confusion and distress until you come home... to a higher consciousness.

Know that all your development will take place in silence.

Much of your growth will be caused by shocks, but your real evolution of spirit will be a silent process.

Your new consciousness will manifest in your surroundings.

As you elevate, so will your setting in life improve.

You may hide and take refuge in the house you have built in silence... the sanctuary within.

"You can have everything if you only know how to ask.

The essence of the desired object is already within yourself.

Be aware that the fruit is already in the seed.

Formulate your images and ask.

Your seed of thought will bud, blossom and bear fruit.

Everything that happens to us is the result of a seed once planted.

Our present experience is the result of past decisions… change your mind today, and you will build your world of tomorrow.

Your mind is your garden… tend it well," they said.

And what of the hereafter? What is beyond this life?

The old ones would soon long for sleep and they whispered, "We go back whence we came.

All is spirit in the end.

We take nothing with us.

The body falls back into the earth and the spirit, rich or poor, lives on.

We all live forever… somewhere."

THE MANA KEEPERS

So tides of conflict have torn at the shores of
your world

And seasons of anguish have left you devoid of
faith and shorn of dreams

And life has become grey and tastes like ashes

And advice from others gives no answers and
no comfort…

Then break the binding chains of dead words
and dare to walk into the unknown

For in letting go, your life will be simplified

And spectres of the past will begin to fade

Then you will feel the slow rekindling of old
fires within

For you will look at the world with new eyes

And when you pass through wooded terrain
cooled by the breath of many blossoms

And green lace canopies shade you

And silken quiet presses in like gloved hands
around your ears

You will feel the miracle of new awareness
dawning…

For nature will begin to speak… and ancient
voices will respond inside you

And a long-lost harmony will be restored

Then a new flowering will begin in your mind and heart

And as you blossom… everything around you will burst into celebrations of loud color and mirror back recognition

For all of life is one…

Nothing ever dies

A rainbow may fade… but it is still there… vibrant and colorful in the mind's eye… and so it still exists

A dry leaf drops… but a new green shoot is already sprouting

The sun may set here… but it is already rising somewhere else

Dawn is always hidden in the sunset

And it is only an eclipse that covers your inner sun of faith

Then as if for the first time you will notice the beauty of flowers…

poised in a shimmering haze like a mystical aura

For they bloom out of dank dirt and mud… only to triumph and raise brave bright heads and give freely of their perfume

Breathe it in like mana

And dance like a madman before that array of blossoms

23

For you will see the power called God in the overflow of his life force spilling out in a confetti of satin petals

For as the flowers innocently open and soak in showers of rain that fall like a blessing...

You will open also

And pour out your admiration for the courage of small seeds

For they bare themselves to the elements so they can bloom and grow

Then born from the night... they are nourished only by their faith in the unknown

And so it is with yourself

For you lie becalmed... afraid to plunge deeper into the real substance of life

And you close yourself to all the treasures it has to offer

So your potential never flowers... and you remain just a dead seed for many lifetimes... until you dare to move out of the known

Then journey on... lifted by the joy of new beginnings

Never seek anything

Truth will seek you when you are ready... such is the paradox

And as you listen to the secret language of

nature you will become a partner in some deep mystery of life

And you will live totally in the moment rejoicing in the precious here and now

For there is no need to hurry anything

Learn from nature… she knows no time limits

But waits without anxiety while everything unfolds in its own time and in its own way without the pressures of time or worry or age

And know that when time stops… you stand in the place of God

And you will hear hidden dimensions rustling electric in the atmosphere for you will have touched the infinite

Then when you return to the material world… you will find a completely different place

For as you are reborn into the world… the world will be reborn in you

All will change because you observed the simple faith of flowers

Sense the rare treasure locked away on hidden levels

For it waits to be tapped only by those who can truly see with the inner eyes of the soul

It flows as the legendary "Water of Life" that spirals and channels in varying rhythms through all things

For there is nothing that isn't alive…

Mountains and plants and rainbows and sun and soil and sea… all vibrate with its mystical force

And even silent rocks may be charged with its healing presence by holy hands and carry it for aeons…

And water in all its changing moods is the ancient symbol for this power called mana

It roars in Wailele, the waterfall

And dances in Ua, the rain

And floats in Uhiwai, the mist

And plays in Kahawai, the gentle stream

And speaks in Moana, the brooding ocean

Develop a keen awareness of this supernatural force

Read signs and omens in elemental phenomena

Watch stars burning in the velvet heavens by night

Read the positions of those far beacons for the races of Man are their children

And by day look for shapes in clouds

And the behavior of plants

And the moods of the sea

And garlands of rainbows that circle the talking skies

For all are messengers

26

And all can speak… if you will listen

And know that having attained the high state of life in human consciousness you are given the greatest privilege of all… to gather the power called mana and offer it in prayer… back to its source - the higher power called God

For the mysterious mana holds the key to answered prayers

Drink it in with each breath… for it hums all around you… pulsing under the green mantle of nature and watching in the eyes of flowers

And gradually a new flowering will take place within you…

if you begin to pray frequently

For you will be encouraged by an ancient urge, long buried…

Know that everything should be preceded by prayer… then the way is cleared for progress

And answers long sought will come to you

Even though the altar on which you place your hands may be weather-beaten rock and not polished marble… still the same God will respond to you

Then look to the world of people for other fountains…

Give love and compassion and hospitality and trust to all that you meet. . .

For mana will be returned to you on the river of life

Breathe your words into God

Visualize your desires and offer the picture along with your gift of mana

And see it rising like gilded vapor

And soon the rain of blessings will fall in response

For in that magic moment… the mana flows two ways… to the source and back again

Pray constantly to keep your levels of mana high

Take your share of the Wai Ola; fabulous food of the spirit

For it is the gift of the creator to his child

You are not forgotten…

See that the loss of personal mana always results in illness

But the imbalanced body can be corrected by the use of herbs: gifts of the earth

Talk things out with the sufferer until his spirit is back on its true course

For both mind and body must be treated

And healing of the spirit must always come first… that is the ancient law of healing

Seek out the most useful plants from the

mountains to the sea

And search the forests and talk to the spirits of plants and trees

And the plant that stands alone… the one with the most perfect form should be the one chosen to give of its essence

For it contains the most mana

And learn patience from a tree…

For it is moved only by the outside force of the wind

And it grows and changes with infinite slowness

And it has learned to accept its limitations and wait…

And marvel at the symbols of the ocean

For a wave at its climax beats against the shore… foaming and sinking its substance into the yielding sands in a glorious re-enactment of procreation

And tides will always govern your life as they ebb and flow

And when clouds of trouble hide your sun… let the friendly ocean cleanse

For burdens may be symbolically dropped into its churning depths and discarded forever as crested young waves rise up and swallow the old...

And the relentless sea dissolves all in preparation for re-birth in a new form when the mana will pour into different molds

For tides bring in bounty... then ruthlessly sweep it out again... only to wash back in with new challenges, new gifts and new dreams... like gems found on a beach

See the eternal pattern...

Flow with life's currents

Dare to ride on bold waves of change... out to uncharted waters

For there will always be singers on the shore to welcome you back to the safe arms of Earth

See that life and love and childbirth and death...

All are steps in time

God plays the music... and the endless dance goes on

And even pre-natal life is an important phase

For the embryo can hear and sense as it readies itself for another cycle of life on Earth... housing the immortal soul as it takes fleshly form once more

Still you may gaze at the movement of stars

and wonder if life is just a momentary state...
only a 'waiting for death'...

And the mind of Man has become obsessed
with time

For time means gain

And so he measures it

And he frets and fumes when it doesn't
move... cannot move at the frenetic pace he
demands

For life itself takes time to experience
everything

It slowly absorbs and moves on...

So, go beyond the limits of this place called
time... inside yourself to new realms of eternity

And you will see that each person is allotted all
the time he needs to grow and expand his
awareness.

Know that everything will unfold it is own time
and in its own way

Let experience become your teacher

And accept that every minute of the rest of your
life will be spent in the future

And no wisdom nor wealth can bring back one
moment from the past...

Stop guilt... for it robs you of life...

For estranged from your spiritual roots, you lead a desperate existence...

Find your true nature and you will be free...

For it is not you who suffers...

Long have you drifted in a desert of torment... separated from your real self... while an actor lived your life... and lived it badly

Only in death can you live...

Be not shaken by these words

For you must suffer the death of the impersonator... an 'ego' that has built up

It must be dissolved before you can enjoy your real life

See that your greatest problem is that you always stand in your own way

Your war is never outside yourself...

It is always within

You are your own friend... and your own enemy

You have searched long... looking for keys...

But you have been seeking only your real self

And when you realize your true nature... new conditions will flood your experience like quiet rain

With closed eyes, silently say the word 'I'...

And you will feel the ego separate from the

eternal presence within you

For the voice of the ego believes it can influence the power called God

But it is not wise enough to manage even one human life…

Subdue the impostor and yield to the gentler voice within

And your consciousness will open

And penalties for past mistakes will be wiped out

For no pain is ever part of the real you…

It is a reaction from the actor, the outraged ego

The high self sits back and watches the play…

For the ego is ignorant of what lies within you: a system that can alter your experience in the outside world… the workings of three separate minds

Focus on these three levels like a sacred trinity

For without their union… no prayer can be answered… no condition can be changed

Understand your lower subconscious mind well

Learn to use it

Cajole it and treat it as a child

It must be controlled… but also befriended

For it can lead you home

33

It is the messenger of God

And telepathy is its only vehicle in reaching the source

You can sense it in your solar plexus and in your intestines...

It has urged you for so long in your selfish life-drives

and tried to live your life for you...

and ignored the presence of a higher being

and trouble has tarnished your life and filled you with sorrow...

For at that level... Man must devour or be devoured... jungle law prevails

For the lower mind is childlike... at an earlier stage of evolution

And it nurtures habits of long standing.

And from it spring the baser aspects of Man

All emotions arise from it

And it harbors deep-seated guilts and fears... some brought over from previous lives

All blockages must be removed from the path

For encumbered, the subconscious cannot do its work of carrying the message to God

The gift of mana and prayer must rise without obstruction on an invisible beam to the higher power where it will materialize...

The subconscious must be taught daily that new ideas are possible

And this task falls to the conscious mind

For it plays the part of a directing parent

It is reasoning and rational and it dwells in the head of a man

And it trains the wayward lower mind in freeing itself of the deadly poison of hatred

Amends must be made for injuries to others

Balance a bad deed of the past with a good deed in the present

And the subconscious will feel cleansed...

The high self is old and wise

It glows over the man like a painted halo in an old icon

It is the great comforter you seek

It is the guardian... and both mother and father; an androgynous parent in whom one can place implicit trust

Man must live under its guidance... as a loving son... if harmonious earthly life is to be found

But for some reason this higher self never descends uninvited...

It waits to be asked in the seeds of prayer...

You wish to learn the truth?

To gain knowledge is the only meaning of life

Know that this 'truth' cannot be taught

You can only experience it

Teach it to yourself by being and knowing

For no man of himself knows anything

No man can perform miracles

But he can elevate his consciousness to receive them

For we are all channels...

And when you admit that you don't know the answer

Then you are ready for the 'truth' to flow in...

For if you are smug and think you know all...

you will close your gates of learning

Human life flows like a river. The world is a river. You are a river...

And consciousness has ebbed and flowed for ages...

And when you bemoan the suffering you have long endured...

Know that the waiting seed needs a struggle to break through its prison of soil... or it can never grow

Learn that nothing is ever really dead

And if you strive, you can escape any prison

But effort is always needed

For, without the problem of reaching for the sunlight… every seed would remain a seed

So resent not your difficulties in the jungle

or your loneliness in the desert

For each state teaches its own lesson

Learn from the kaleidoscope of experiences that colors your life

You need everything that happens to you…

Be a witness to the drama of your life…

For evolution is taking place within you

Your highest self was once an unconscious mind… then a conscious mind… until it reached its present omniscience

And throughout its lifetimes of difficult growth… it has experienced every human condition

So it is greater than any problem you can present to it

It remains unshaken…no matter how desperate the struggles of the man

Go to this higher awareness for help

And let it guide you

For it is your share of the power called God

You are not expected to be simply absorbed
into this thing called God and escape the rigors
of worldly life

You must meet the demands of life in the flesh

And be helpful to all other forms of life around
you

And you may ask for your share of life's
bounty

And the high self will help you attain it

As long as you do not violate the rights or
possessions of another...

For you have long been concerned with only
your immediate problems

And locked on that lower personal level, you
cannot see your place in the wider scheme of
things

Do you not know who you are?

You are one of the Keepers of Earth

And on a higher plane your own consciousness
is combined with all other forms of life...

For once your own earthly vehicle is in order...
you may take your part in the great eternal
scheme

And on that enormous scale it is awesome

For the entire animal, human and plant
kingdoms unite in one vast awareness

Rejoice in the beauty of this planet you call

home

Look again at its mighty oceans reflecting heavenly lights

Enjoy its changes of season from sun to snow

Penetrate its deep green forests seething with hidden forms of life

Inhale its plants and flowers as they burst in riots of color when their seasons come

The earth is a mass of sensitivities

But Man has become insensitive to its needs

For he wallows in the weak processes of his own small sphere

And he has drifted far from the life-force

And he hears not the cry of nature…

The earth itself has a soul… it is alive and sensitive… and not just a dry clump of soil

It is a body. It breathes: It lives.

And it carries Man along like a great protective ship in space.

Look to a crystal stream

Be absorbed in its water

For you are it and it is you

And so it is with the power called God

You are not separate or alone but a part of each other

Your search is merely God in search of himself

And when water is disturbed

And mud is stirred up spoiling its purity

You need only wait and be patient

Stand aside as a stranger watching from the banks

And soon the dirt will settle to the bottom

And the stream will flow on unclouded again

For every condition passes

Know that you will not step into the same water twice

By allowing outside events to fall in and disturb the clarity of your mind… you are disturbing yourself

Silently listen and you will be washed with these words

For they will ring like energies of God striking chords inside you

Echoes of something once known and long forgotten

Open your heart to understanding and find your true self

It is the first step to lifting the veil of bad dreams you thought was life

For, without your own peace of mind you cannot help another

A seeker is like a delicate young sapling needing protection as it grows

And when you become a great strong tree... bearing fruit and offering shade to others... you will be invulnerable to the disturbances of this world

Your strength will grow by degrees as you make your journey...

Awaken to the miracle of a new viewpoint

Look again at the parched desert your life has become...

But this time... look with different eyes

And see not barrenness and death

but seeds waiting under that sandy soil for the gift of water to raise them to life

And soon the empty plain will be ablaze with blossoms... because of the faith of seeds

And have you not sensed the thrilling spell of the woodland as you walk through its shafts of mystical light?

For you will hear the music of the oldest religion... if you listen to the wind making tall trees sing

And you will see ancient pictures in the flames

that leap from crackling logs on a bonfire

And you will hear unearthly voices in the roar
of the sea when bold waves break on sandy
shores…

And have you not marvelled at a waving field
of golden wheat?

Or yellow daffodils nodding beside a calm lake
in springtime?

Or succulent red fruits hanging full and ripe on
stout trees?

For nature gives generously of its bounty… and
asks no reward

And the part that is best in you responds with
bursts of joy

For it is God flowering

And God bearing fruit

And God's voice in the sea and on the wind

And God's face in the flames…

Listen well… for all the sounds of nature are
basically the same…

the music of the sea… the blowing of the
wind… the burning of a fire…

All contain the original humming sound of life
itself

And if you carry distress from your dealings with the world of people

And if you have been almost destroyed by the pain of relationships

And your trust has always ended in betrayal

And you long to be free of the nightmares that lurk behind human involvement...

Look again to your own view of things

If someone lets you down... cease to see him as you want him to be

Put aside the picture you have painted of your friend

And let the true person gradually emerge...

Then you will be spared the pangs of disappointment...

"Conflict is natural... neither positive or negative...

It is merely patterns of energy interfering with each other

Nature uses conflict as a major power for change

And with it she creates canyons and mountains and pearls

Consider not that you have conflict in your life...

But what you do with it..."

"And it is not required to love everyone… just
to be in a loving state of mind… not a hating
state

For love is a breathing of the soul

And you must breathe, even if your enemy is
there

And in love your spirit can be born

Love is timelessness… thoughts cease.

And without thinking… lost in love… you
are…

For all human suffering is caused by a wrong
outlook towards events…

or the expectation of too much from others

For your delusions will clash with the reality of
things

Strive to keep a balance in your feelings

Centre yourself on the wheel of life

Be neither excited over success… nor deflated
when you lose

And be not perplexed by duality

For nothing exists without its opposite

Everything needs a comparison

For every enjoyment there will be
disillusionment

You will meet with friendliness… and you will face hostility

Some will love you, while others curse your name

You are in bondage to the world of people when you look to them for the benevolence and compensation that can only come from the power called God

Neither justice nor recognition nor gratitude can come from anywhere else…

And in your lack of confidence, you gather the opinions of others…

But opinion is not knowledge

Why be disturbed by what others say?

They are as fragile as you are… buffeted themselves by the storms of life

The whims of society matter not

You know who you are

But each person will view you differently according to the aperture of his vision

Know yourself… and be free of the labels placed on you…

Control your attention

Centre it not on the failures of others…

Or your own limitations and fears…

Or the difficulty of the moment that presses

you down like an iron hand

But lift your consciousness toward the spiritual
fountain within

And you will be safe

Let old concepts fall away

And give no energy to thoughts that haunt you
from the dead past

They cannot replay if they are given no
power...

Face your problems

And learn to blame yourself for your troubles...
and not the outside world

For your mind is the eye through which you
view life

Guard it well lest it color your vision of the
truth

For there are scars on every mind

We all hurt from unhealed wounds

Have the courage to call back these situations

And relive the events that cloud your mind

Call up the desires you had at the time...
however violent they may be

You wanted to kill... or you wanted to love

Re-enact the entire play... but this time be
undisturbed by it

Re-create the situation… but this time control it

And old injuries will heal

Let not the dust of the past cloud your vision of
the present

Let not others daunt you by word or deed…

For you will meet with people at every level of
incarnation

Some are new to the human realm… and
predatory in their habits

And they manifest the lower traits of savagery,
greed and cowardice

But you will also meet with more advanced
souls… returning to Earth again and again… to
learn their lessons and burn out their egos while
growing back towards the source

Condemn not anyone you meet…

But strive to understand his actions instead

Observe the various stages of human
development…

For all have the same structure within:…
complexes to be removed before they can
ascend to a higher thought-world

Learn compassion towards all

No one can harm you or impede your course…
although in their ignorance some will try…

Read people well

Study their many facets and learn from them

Step aside and travel on...

The seasons of your experience come and go

You will move forward... then you will slip back

But no one is ever really lost

And if you expect happiness when living with another...

Know that there are two other people who always come between a couple:

two false selves who stand in the way

So the two real people can never meet, unless they are looking within themselves at the same time

Learn to live in the same thought-world as your partner...

And friction will dissolve

And if you feel becalmed

And your life has stopped...

Know that you will only move forward by casting useless things aside

Drop your worn-out attitudes of the past

For there can be no progress until you change

As your thoughts become new... so do your

circumstances

You cannot grow if your mind is poisoned by negativity

Let a new state break through into your awareness

And cling not to your old familiar misery afraid to let go, lest you drown in the sea of the unknown...

For change is not loss

Find your own secret reflections

And polish the mirror of faith daily... lest it become dull and tarnished

Learn from the mirror

It never knows anything

It is simply waiting in the present... ready to reflect

Know that if you focus on God... he will focus on you

And once you truly perceive your deep inner world...

your life will be instantly transformed

The old self will dissolve in a flash of insight

And old bitterness of the past will fade from your experience

And friends and relatives will become completely different people

And familiar surroundings will become completely different places

For wrong opinions and false ideas are easier to see

They lie close to the surface

But the truth lies in the depths and is harder to find

And know that the roots of certain words contain keys to unlock the mystery of Man and guide him through the perilous span of earthly life

and foster him while ever rising on the eternal spiral

For some words are heavily charged with mana

And when something is said… its existence has begun

And angry words are angry actions… they are forces in themselves

While words of inspiration and hope are as spurs for the inner man

For words have the power of life and death locked up in their roots

And the spoken word can never be retrieved

So remember everything…

Poetry was the answer to the people of old

For beautiful words are easily retained in the mind

And repetition forms a bridge for the memory

And when you breathe your prayers with force to that highest God of power... power that hums through the spiritual channel in the song of the wind from the sun... the realization of the One Great God Above All will flood over you

And you will know that there is only one temple that Man can truly build

And it is made of intangible materials: love and happiness and faith and prayer

And no outside hands can ever pull it down

Forgive those that have harmed you in the past and vow to help them instead of seeking revenge

And hostility will fade from your aura

And harmony will flood back to you as the message shakes your inner being:

Compassion is all

Be aware of the journey right through to the beyond... the state after death

And see that as generation follows generation, some move out into the light as they float and circle silently... ever rising on the ascending spiral... each consciousness growing and expanding according to the lessons of life...

And if a loved one is dying… ask him to examine the attitudes he carries with him

Urge him to shed the remorse and the anger and the dreads of this life

And his path will be easier in the next

Know that death is not the end… but merely a change of form: the beginning of a new cycle…

Mourn not the traveller who passes… but rejoice with him as he releases the burdens of this harsh life and soars high towards his rebirth… his new body… his new mind…his new fortune…

The song of life can never end

For the only fear of death is in leaving the known and the familiar

Try dying every day to your old self… so that you emerge renewed and young again as the tired mind sheds it load…

And guard against false laws provided by the ego…

Think not that everyone should love you

Or that you must not fail

Or that you must worry about the problems of another

Or that you need a stronger person to rely on

Or that you must explain your life to
everybody…

Free yourself from these chains

Face your unhappiness

Then examine the state with curiosity

And when looked at truthfully… it will fade

And if people would tear you down

Launch a constructive rebellion against them

Do not try to please them

For if you no longer seek their approval… they
have no power over you

Retain your individuality

Do not expect criticism… and it will seldom
appear

Do not resist… for you may distort the facts

And our of fear you may create opposition
where none is needed…

Look into yourself… although it may cause you
pain

Be courageous

Face your faults and know their names

For they are impediments on your path to God

In past times they were known as sin…

Jealousy… greed… intolerance and egotism…

All will block your way to answered prayers

Eradicate them

And there are seekers who have sailed in rough waters…

For in passing from one incarnation to another…

Some males must acquire the qualities of females

And some females must adopt the traits of men

And the world of people does not understand…

Minds and bodies are melting into each other before ultimately uniting in the highest consciousness… with the character of both sexes

For each individual lives in a world of his own making…

There are as many worlds as there are minds

And there are worlds within worlds

It is a multitude of levels…apart and yet joined…

It is a mystery

The bird knows nothing of the world of the fish

And the fish knows nothing of the world of plants

Yet all are nourished by one great universal power

For the power called God is both father and mother to all who seek it

And apart from some physical features... there is no difference between man and woman as they incarnate

They are molded from the same essence

They are of the same mind... the same degrees of intelligence

And both have access to the same spiritual source

For the aim of all seekers is to purify the mind in order to reveal the spirit which is neither male nor female...

The search takes one above body and mind

Study the many worlds of animals and learn from them

For they can teach us much that the human race has forgotten

The dog remains loyal... even to those who have mistreated him

And he acts not out of stupidity... but from a seemingly deep understanding of human shortcomings

Examine your own patterns of disloyalty… to yourself and others

Are you becoming mean and critical because of the company you are keeping?

Always return kindness when it is given from the heart

And reinforce the golden chains of friendship… for they carry much mana for the giver and the receiver

Examine carefully your dark thought-forms for they may be telling you wrongly that you are not worthy of loyalty to yourself or others

Wipe out these adversaries to your confidence

And marvel at the whale

For it carries records from the past and it reminds us that sound frequencies can bring up memories of ancient knowledge

And learn from the dolphin for it knows that the rhythms of life are to be found in breathing

For it measures its breath before submerging

And it knows the ancient language of sounds and it communicates with nature

Realign yourself with these universal tides

And release old breath and with it old stress

Then breathe deeply and taste the vitality of renewed mana

And you may envy the world of animals in the wild

For their lives are so simple beside that of Man with his constant mind-tortures

and his crowded living and his feverish striving for wealth

For the wild animals' lives are concerned only with the basics of living…

keeping warm or keeping cool or feeding or reproducing their young… and then dying with a minimum of fuss when their cycles end… to make way for other generations to take their places

Uncomplaining, the animals fit into the great scheme of life

While Man frets and doubts everything about his existence from the cradle to the grave

For Man's heightened intellectual and imaginative powers have brought him nothing but irrational fears and searing emotional responses that animals lack… and are better off without

And the butterfly reminds us of the art of transformation

For it takes many forms before it flies

And so it is with your ideas:

See them first as eggs… then larvae… then cocoons until the ideas are completed and born into material form

And look to the wild birds which beautify the environment

Observe how they reach for freedom… soaring upward to great heights as far as their strength will allow… with the blue sky as their only limit

Learn from them and go as high as you can

Simplify your life

Rest yourself from personal trials and complications

Look to this planet which is sadly in need of attention

Show it the respect it deserves

For there are people in high places who would destroy it

And their heads are full of their hunger for power

And their folly knows no bounds

For their weapons could cause a winter from which mankind would never emerge

And the earth's delicate ecosystem would be mortally wounded…

For already there are cold silent places… once loud with multitudes of feathered creatures chirping excited notes of life

And darting from branch to branch in celebration… wrapped in the safe foliage of familiar trees

But now, small, still bodies litter the ground where they've fallen…

Some brown with white throats… some speckled… some shiny blue-black…

others splashed with red feathers on weakened wings as they gasp in the agonized tremors of slow death

For birds return to favorite haunts with no expectation of the evil awaiting them when all plantlife has been sprayed

As Man sallies forth on a crusade against the diseases of trees

And innocents are poisoned as they eat of their natural food

For the noxious substance spares nothing

It reaches insects lurking in dark nooks on the bark of trees

And it strikes earthworms tunneling into once safe soil

And green places become burial grounds

And mornings are silent now without birdsong…

And look to streams where fish lay dead and dying on the banks

Some distorted unimaginably by hideous growths projecting from silver bodies, once sleek and swift

And now some rivers are dank and dead

For all life has been stilled in them by the oozing of chemical wastes spilled out of industrial plants upstream

And helpless marine species are forced to dwell in toxic waters

While the mindless wheels of the commercial world grind blissfully on...

See that Man is throwing the shadow of sterility over all living things

For the poison he spreads kills without discrimination

And its victims are nature's own safeguards

For birds will normally keep the number of insects in check

But if they are sabotaged, nature is thrown out of balance

Help the balance... without destroying it

For predatory species will always keep other numbers down...

It is the pattern from the beginning of time

For nature speaks…

It has no words… it uses signs

If you are near trees… become a tree… feel its vibrant life

Sense the sweet sap coursing through its trunk and branches

Inhale the scent of flowers arround you… become a blossom

Walk into the ocean… taste its salt… feel its mighty force sweep over your body… know that you are one with it

And as Man you are expected to influence other life-streams positively

For when less developed entities come within your sphere of love and respect… both of you will advance spiritually

And you will gain mana

And see the outer universe as a constantly changing process of material forms

And so it is with the inner world of Man

For he fantasizes through a variety of impressions and emotions

And thoughts and feelings are the finer forms of matter moving in a shifting mosaic

See that old opinions can be removed

For you are not the same person you were a moment ago

And time knows nothing

Only the inner self is aware

Focus on that realization… for out of it come answers to the enigma of life

And know that you can rely on nothing but ever-changing change

And there are some eyes you can never meet for fear of seeing your own image

For accumulated hurts and feelings build up to bursting point

Until you lash out at friend or lover or parent or child

And you blame the other… and never yourself

And you hold outsiders responsible for your own inner pain

And your self-image clashes with the reality

And the conflict is so painful that you can barely stay alive

But clinging to false beliefs you live on somehow and avoid the truth that could set you free

And illusion flourishes

For it is built on nothing but ego: the false self…

Learn to live… just simply live

For in childhood you knew how to enjoy and be happy…

Then the hypnotism of the world set in

And as an adult you became misguided…

Face the fact of your lost happiness

And the appalling chill of loneliness

And a better state will return…

Just let life happen in a natural way

Do not object and do not resist

Fret over nothing

Then you will feel the effortless, timeless flow of life

Do not carry… and you will be carried

Then on days when rainbows arch across leaden skies… rejoice as you read their symbols

See that life is not just one color… but seven like the bands of the rainbow

Life can never be just one calm shade… it always has many facets

And a strange wisdom will come to you if you put your mind aside and just be

Be not afraid of the vast sea of untraveled consciousness within you as you dare to dredge up floods of lost knowledge from the past

Be not afraid to fall too deeply into emptiness
as you move into the unknown and the dread of
nothingness shakes you to the core

Fear not the loss of your identity

For within, you are neither man nor woman

And you have no race nor color nor creed

For life should be an intoxicating mystery to be
drunk in and enjoyed… not just a confusing
puzzle or a dark morass of uncertainty

See that none of your fabled teachers or your
brilliant philosophers have altered your
sorrow…

So never follow another

Rely on no one

Look into yourself for all the answers…

For you have long blamed the world and not
yourself for your troubles

But pain arises only from your own confusion

The world is neutral

You can make what you want out of it

See it as a testing ground for your personal
growth

For when a fruit is still green... it clings to the branch of the tree

And if the fruit is pulled off while green... it is not ready... and it hurts

And so it is with you and the Tree of Life...

Stick with the tree

Gain all the experience it can give you...

For you will drop off when you are mature and ready

Man himself is the Tree of Life

What you have been seeking... you already have

For all paths lead home to the inner self

You can teach yourself by being and knowing

You do not need any deeper mysteries to be shown to you

Simply accept your own awareness and live in the moment

Do not miss the now

You will not find God by escaping from the world.

but by diving deeper and deeper until you find him at the very core of your existence... God is hidden there

For in dreaming of shining trees outside

yourself… you miss the search… the opportunity for growth in this lifetime

You are the tree… and you have all levels of consciousness lying dormant inside you like seeds awaiting rain…

Since the birth of thought, Man has been the leading shoot on the Tree of Life

For once… maybe only once… in the course of its existence has the earth enveloped itself with life and with thought

There may be only one season…

So learn all you can

For Man is irreplaceable

He represents the most synthesized state under which the stuff of life is available

He is the key to the whole science of nature…

And if you ache from loneliness…

Know that Man apparently wanders homeless on the face of the earth

Trees have roots… birds have nests… animals have lairs and caves

And nature succors them and even rejoices through them

as flowers bloom and birds sing and young animals romp in their vitality

But the serious human thinks he needs a family
to survive

And he seeks the props of society to lean on

And he dreads to stand alone

And he feels like a stranger on this planet

So he uses religion as a home and a retreat

And his search for something called 'Truth'
becomes his comfort

For nationalities have divided the races of Man
and caused fear

And that fear has made Man aggressive

And living in that fear he can never pursue
'Truth'…

And so he lives… afraid of yesterday, today,
and tomorrow… overlooking all that the
present has to offer

And claiming to be the highest species… Man
expects petty rewards for everything he does

Learn from nature… it gives freely. It
sacrifices. That is the law of life.

A tree brings forth fruit… does it demand that
you give it water?

The plant simply blossoms, gives out its
fragrance and dies when its time is over

Know that you will not find a heaven by roaming to far, exotic places on this earth

You need only the movement that has begun in your consciousness...

Stretch into God by inward gazing

Work with your triune nature

And you will make your own heaven wherever you go

And when you weary of the world

And your senses desire a different experience

Do not ease your pain with something artificial... something on which you may grow to rely

For the substance may fill you with a false sense of elation which is only temporary...

For only the ego is a slave to your addictions

Would you want the delusion that you are doing better than you are?

Why settle for the imitation when you could have the real thing?

Use your natural awareness...

Open yourself to the miracle of life going on all around you

Sense your intimate part in the great scheme of it all...

And you will soar higher than you have ever been

The work you have chosen does not hinder your private journey…

Farmers and philosophers… peasants and patriarchs… all have the same goal

It is a quiet knowledge and a secret quest

And if you observe one who makes an elaborate show of his supposed inward grace…

Know that he is not as far along the path as he would have others think

And if you would feel a link with your source…

still your senses… one by one

Neither see, nor touch, nor taste, nor smell

And imagine yourself being drawn into a dark, silent vale within…

Let go of all sensations of the outside world

Sounds are the last to leave

And as they fall away… you will float within… to a great stream of eternal consciousness that courses through you and all living things

Feel that you are one with it…

And you will touch God in the region of your heart

For in looking inward… you have also ascended

And because you appear different from the crowd...

the voices of the world may speak against you...

Know that slander and gossip cannot destroy you

Bend like the willow

And let the flood of criticism wash over you

For only the ego will be bruised

And when the water recedes... your real self will still stand... untouched and unspoilt

And if your spoken prayers to an unseen God have long been unanswered...

Know that words of themselves are empty...

There are no magic phrases... no secret names of God... only silent words charged with the force called mana

Make your own statements of power and offer them to the subconscious mind

For this is the only effective method of spoken prayer

And as you reach new plateaux of thought

And old friends drop away...

Fear not loneliness

For there is a silent communication between

those at the same level of awareness

And for the first time you will not be lonely…

And when you re-enter the world of people…
you will encounter the same obstacles and
heartaches and negativities that have bogged
you down in the past…

But this time, see through their illusion and free
yourself from that level of thought

Know that all the waters of the oceans are the
same waters

And so it is with this thing called "Truth"

For many teachers may bring it to you… but it
is always the same truth

For its seeds will be blown everywhere

Some will fall on hard stone

But a mind may carry that seed to more fertile
soil…

And so someday it is sown…

Awaken to your true nature

Observe the world with new eyes

Drink in your new knowledge

Yet you may still feel empty…

Know that in emptiness you come closest to the
source of your being

For once the conscious, reasoning mind is
devoid of any concept… the feeling of God is
then able to enter…

Fear not the dark, frightening vacuum that
yawns inside you

But see it as a womb from which all can be
born

And in the rose-pink light of morning when
fragrant blossoms drip from trees… symbols of
your new knowledge

You will look deeper into all that surrounds
you

And you will know that we all live on islands
of time watched by the eye of God

And ultimately… nothing matters

So your quest has brought you far

And you have shed old guilts and thoughts like
worn-out cloaks

And the fabric of your life has been unravelled

And you have been shattered

But new knowledge has built you up again

And you have been led back to the guidance of
your higher self

And you feel the aeons of experience stretching
behind you and far ahead

And you hear the whisper of past homecomings echo inside you…

as your trinity unites once more

And your ancient links are renewed with planet Earth

You changed… for you cannot die

And now as you walk into a new sun…

Look over your shoulder…

And all that you seek will follow like your shadow

THE FIRE LILY

Do not live like most people…

And you will not cry like them

Rise above wrong ideas that you have cherished

No longer fight to defend false notions that fill your days with misery.

Search deep within your heart

And find the ancient fire that can burn away any obstacles that hinder your path to peace.

Still you will meet with the ignorant who always fight facts

Let them cling to their self-defeating opinions.

For you can welcome the glow of self-enlightenment

And bask in the knowledge that there is another way of being…

Let go of past bitterness

And choose the freedom of now

For you are not your mind or your memories or thought-pictures that torment you

You are an undying spirit that can be fanned like a fire and renewed.

Let the maelstrom of set-backs sweep over you…Be unaffected.

Just see it as a texture of life.

Cling to nothing, but renounce. Burn out the dross and place yourself in a state of non-attachment to people, places and things...

Give your fire its chance to heal you.

Then you will gradually feel a tremendous sense of purity...like a white lily blooming.

The flame will transform into a lily.

In its own silent place, flowers the fiery lily of eternal renewal...

Your fire. Your lily...

You can never die...only change.

So anger has brought you this far...

And only a miniscule thread of dwindling faith keeps you going from day to bleak day.

And dark dawns and darker sunsets bring reminders of the pain your family inflicted... intentionally or unintentionally...

And the child still cries inside you; angry and hurt over what your parents didn't give when you longed for their understanding or comfort or begged for their protection.

Know that they may wish they could have acted differently

And would, if they had another chance

But they too were caught up in their own problems

Every family has a story…

So you dealt with your suffering by retreating and covering up or converting one feeling into another and somehow you survived.

Know that hostility will steal your life if you let it

Do not feel threatened or undermined by all you have had to endure

For what you think of yourself is only imagined anyway: a thought-image is not the real you.

Live the life you have been handed… for you earned it during countless incarnations on the endless spiral.

Learn from it. See it as a teacher

For whatever has the power to distress, can also heal.

Be glad that you have been given another chance to work out your deepest attachments and imbalanced emotions in yet another lifetime…

For if certain patterns of thought or action could be expressed without pain or difficulty, then how could you learn from them?

You would just continue to act out old habits, without any reflection or self-examination…

For negative blockages carry over from past lives

Use this time around to work out those
obstacles to your progress

And look to your attachments in this life, for
they may cause imbalance

Free yourself from unhealthy needs for they are
blocking your path to transformation

And some will not find it easy to escape from
attachments… to people, places and things.

For attachment can take many deceptive forms.

Do not fight it… but understand it.

For inside yourself, so much may be missing,
that you cling to anything and anyone in order
to feel safe.

Being without roots, you try to convert
anything into your roots.

Know that when you find your true inner self,
you will know at last who you are; the being
and consciousness inside you will shine forth
and you will be rooted in that and never cling
to anything or anyone outside yourself again.

Fear not that becoming rooted in yourself, you
will be unable to love.

For only then will you be truly able to give
love.

You will share, with no conditions and no
expectations

For you will have an abundance inside you;

The overflowing of your inner self is love.

Only a higher answer can solve your problems...

But you desperately seek other solutions that will please you...

So that the wrong in you will seem right.

And you are doomed by your despair and frustration as you seek that pleasing answer...

And so you stagger on... drained by people and worn down by conditions.

And no one seems able to offer any real help

And you burn from the feeling of being cheated, left out and overlooked

And the hollow prospect pervades; that tomorrow will be just as pointless and empty as today...

For you are always undermined by your own sense of insecurity...

Sabotaged by yourself, in all that you do.

Know that the only reason your life is so dismal is because you think you cannot do any better.

Be heartened... for you can control your thoughts in any situation.

Think in a higher way

And new life will flood your experience as the rising of a new sun gilds the earth

Wait for the Fruit of Return...

For we all sing to something lost

And the memory of it rings in our blood:

The glowing of an unchanging fire within.

Know that from the loss of innocence can come new growth and new beginnings.

And new life arises from purification by fire...

The bloom of the Fire Lily.

Listen to the laughter of her flames.

For she will be born of your suffering.

As you burn in guilt and anger

And rage in envy and greed

And waste your substance in the pursuit of desires which bring only short-lived comfort.

And estranged from your spirit-fire, you wander aimlessly without roots

And you never feel that you belong in this world.

Know that strong habits and patterns of the past exert such a strong pull, that they must be replaced by something stronger.

Fire flares up high into the sky

And reaches the point beyond which the flame

cannot retain its own nature

So it converts into smoke…

Elevate your level of being

And change will be inevitable.

Be completely honest

Dare to open up and see yourself as you really are

Then show your true self to those you meet

And like a lily that folds itself inwards at night

You will unfold in the day and show yourself to the outside world

And from within, you will give compassion and understanding to others

And your heart will connect with other beating hearts

For only when you are balanced and centered yourself, will you be open and honest with others

Ponder the depths of your own heart

Examine the desires and intentions you find there.

Are they pure?

What harm would they cause yourself and others if they were fulfilled?

Let the mirror of life reflect the essence of yourself

Let your own inner workings be the new direction you will take.

For, physically and spiritually you are an important part of the great wheel of life that turns endlessly

Do not waste this incarnation in frivolity.

Play your part well and be the best that you can be.

Balance yourself on the wheel of life

Be emotionally, physically and spiritually centered

For imbalance causes tension, fear and uncertainty-and you will not go forward into the good that awaits you.

Move with the grace of a bird in flight.

Stretch inside yourself and find your balanced position and you will feel a deep healing.

For there are times in your life when you are empty…

Pain is an emptiness you must face

But know that it allows you to be filled with other gifts of the spirit

Every pain has a purpose.

You must work through the discomfort and

suffering in order to go beyond the range of ordinary experience… surpassing all other limits

You need the pain.

It is a mountain to be climbed and overcome.

Accept your problems… for they are inevitable

See those obstacles in another way

And gain strength in overcoming them.

Let them push you higher than you've ever been

Empty yourself of suffering and fill yourself with joy in the endless dance of life.

For life is loss; a constant emptying of ourselves… so that we may be refilled

See the various stages of personal loss for what they are… accept them.

For peace will soon fill your void

And you will soar into renewal of the spirit…

Gratitude will balance regret

Fear not that others may see through you and expose the false inner condition that keeps you hanging in shreds…

What if they do?

They are probably just as uncertain themselves, aching for a sense of security just as you are.

The only way to abolish the discovery and exposure of the false inner self… is to get rid of the falseness.

For you are false because you have not found understanding of your true nature.

Know that nothing evil and nothing wrong is ever part of your real self, but only a masquerade…

Let the falseness fall from you like dry, parched leaves.

And if you have a morbid attachment to your pattern of gloom

And the chilling fear that you are doomed plays at the edge of all your activities like a tattered ghost…

See the pain and illusion of it all… and free yourself

Do not be gullible… think for yourself

Do not follow the dictates of society…

For shallow opinions steer you away from the path of truth and muffle the inner voice you desperately need to hear.

Remove yourself… sing your secret songs and bring magic and wonder back into your world

You may find that you know more melodies than you thought you did… if you open your heart to hear the haunting music of its sadness

For your sorrow will flow away on its refrain

And loosen the tight bands inside you

And set them free on the air

Into the dark night which will heal you…

For, from darkness everything is born.

And when a moon of omens rises…

Know that somewhere your voice will always be heard

For there is no real death

An echo of your special music will remain wherever you have been

A song can set you free

Forgiveness brings freedom from pain.

All your prayers and good works mean nothing until you forgive those around you for what might have been…

Then, forgive yourself… and move on into new experience and renewed life.

Forgive and release anyone who has bombarded you with bad words or arrows of unkind thoughts.

For we all have notions of what should be corrected in others… their faults and their vices.

Instead, clarify your own consciousness.

React no longer to issues of the past… cease to dwell in old pain.

But live and act in the present.

Let go of thoughts, actions, opinions and attitudes that are no longer beneficial for your continued growth.

Cast aside the negativity that has kept you separated from communion with your inner voice; the voice of the spirit.

Let go of the illusion of loneliness and enjoy solitude, so that you can hear the voice of your own heart…

For it will teach you much.

Do not love your hell…

Observe that many will scream and plead for release from mental agony… but they don't mean it.

They love their own private hells…

Their agonies are precious possessions, not to be given up lightly.

And distress is a taste of excitement they cannot live without…

Hell is nowhere but inside yourself

Your own negativity is a hell

And so are your evil desires and self-obsession…

Learn how to empty yourself of life's distractions, so you can fill up with eternal knowledge

For there is no such thing as time or age in eternity... just the moment.

Cleanse yourself of careless tendencies for they rob you of opportunities that may never come around again.

Avoid the misuse of power in matters of sex or relationships

Let past upheavals dissipate and a healing, resting period will descend on those areas of your life which have brought turmoil

Expand your horizons...

Let your energy open to receive new seeds and you will find a new way of being

And when the crescent of a new moon adorns the velvet night...

Plant your dreams and goals

And wherever you see beauty, be reminded of the power called God...

In the sunset... in the song of a bird... the fragrance of a flower... the dance of water in a stream... the grace of an animal... a human face... there is a temple of God in that beauty.

For all other temples are man-made and God cannot be found there.

But when soaring mountains pierce the clouds and the wind sings an ancient song through the trees… God is found in those temples.

For he has made them. Drink in the beauty for it is a prayer.

Beauty is everywhere if you look with new eyes.

So it is a constant prayer. And that continual undercurrent of communion with God, can transform your life…

For wisdom can help you transcend humanity and its conditions and enter into the world of the divine.

But know that wisdom is not knowledge or inspiration; it is a phenomenal entity that grows in the heart

It is the growth of love… and love brings insight; a different kind of knowing

For it makes you aware of things which cannot be seen with ordinary eyes. You will see what cannot be seen; hear what cannot be heard…

Love makes the impossible, possible… Learn to love your life

Mere knowledge is ordinary… but wisdom of the heart is a miracle.

For it is so easy to journey through life reacting to every outside force that you encounter.

And blindly, you align with the roles your family, culture and gender have dictated to you

And although you are unique as a human entity, still you battle with inner conflicts and secret fears

And you stagger along, unsure of who you are or what you really want

And your life has become simply an act

For, daily, you play your part… following your familiar script…

And under it all, an inner voice screams inside you, longing to be heard: the sound of your true self…

Know that you are more resilient than you think…

Rekindle the old fires of hope, adaptability and control that burn deep inside you.

Some may just glow like fading embers but they are still alive…

Do not be passive anymore, but take an active stance in your life

Take charge of your problems

For there is nothing that cannot be changed or

resolved through persistent effort.

And you have wells of inner strength that you haven't even tapped.

You are here today… that took strength

You made it through the roughest of times… that took strength…

For the human body is the temple in which the endless, ancient struggle takes place: good against evil… light against darkness.

The being known as Man has been sick for so long and he knows it.

For institutions such as family and religion seem to lie in ruins.

And they could have remained sacred if only their laws had been adapted to the real goals of human existence:

Freedom and awareness of a universal harmony of which men and women are an integral part.

For there are two destinies in the entity called Man:

One is a fruit that can perish

And the other is an ancient seed of intelligence which has limitless possibilities: The Seed of The Fire Lily

Man's evolution is eternal.

For you see the world by the reflected light of yourself and illumination arises from the heart…

And as Man blazes on fiery jets into the future and physically stands on new worlds… what will he take with him?

… The ideas he has about his own level of consciousness and the image in which he visualizes the power called God

And his opinions will clash with the God-ideas of other places and other dimensions and other realities which hopefully will be conducive to higher planes of thought…

For, in his new home, Man will evolve into another being, shaped by alien atmospheres and pressures and dreams

And old Earth will be just a faint green patch of memory buried inside him

And he will teach his children carefully, knowing they carry the seeds of tomorrow. He will teach them the wisdom of confronting inner shadows and show them the glorious possibility of resurrection; a sun rising within.

The future of the species rests in these courageous explorers of inner worlds and outer worlds; the sun-eaters.

You are the past

You are the present

You are the future

And you have the power to regenerate yourself

But only by seeing your own existence can you
come to life

Then you will be born again and again...
higher or lower as your heart dictates

You have inside you all the possibilities of
knowledge

Every answer waits there

And your only instructor is yourself

For, without going abroad, you can see all

And the farther you stray from the journey
within... the less you know

This life may bring many eclipses of your inner
sun

For you cannot begin to rework old patterns
until you are conscious of your burning anger
and learn to redirect it

And you cannot create a life of satisfaction
until you are conscious of your fears.

Move through them and quiet them

For often you are afraid without knowing it

And afraid, you remain unaware of your fear

For you have structured your life to suppress intolerable anxiety

And you avoid unfamiliar situations… lest you reawaken traumatic feelings

And you often turn your hidden fears into addictions or compulsions or obsessions

Still, food or money or work or sex give no real comfort

And you stagger on, plagued by psychosomatic ailments, converting fear into anger and anger into aggression as you strive for fame or wealth

And you whip yourself into feverish caprice and unpredictability

And your nerves grow raw from your drive for excitement and passion and change…

Know that it is only your mental self that alters with every changing thought

For one moment you think you know who you are

And the next moment you doubt your identity

Shed such madness

Find the inner peace of your spiritual self

For it dwells in changeless reality and has no doubts…

Let the noise of your mind be still

Then the sacred part in you will be heard…

It carries the message by which you will be
saved

And some will take the secret fire and hide it
away within

It lives in eyes and it lives in hearts

And it can be rekindled from long-dead ashes

For throughout all one's incarnations some
fires went out…

Some were extinguished

And some simply lie like smouldering
embers…

See the sunrise and sunset of this world of
troubles

Watch the flowering of the bud of truth

Drink in its secret smile

For tomorrow it will turn to dust…

And know that the goal of liberation from pain
lies not in escape from the world… but by
becoming enlightened to its mysteries

The horizon symbolizes the world within and
the world without

And the line connecting noon and midnight is

imaginary but its effects are real in the unique star-pattern which distinguished you at birth

For this vertical divider; the meridian separates your birthchart into eastern and western sections… half the visible sky and half the invisible one

And each has a distinct significance…

And in the heart of the east is a single symbolic event that unlocks the meaning of everything… dawn

So horizon and meridian are two natural incisions

And each sunders the prime symbol; the circle

As the sky is cut into two hemispheres

representing the inner world which is hidden…

and the outer world which is visible

The meridian denotes freedom and fate, the absolute power of will and its inevitable collision with other wills… equally free and powerful

And together horizon and meridian form a cross; the cross of life; the cross on which spirit is crucified before there can be a resurrection

Personal action or inaction are critical in shaping the tone of your life

You create your own destiny

Consider the other half of the sky… half of the circle

For in terms of color, sundown is indistinguishable from dawn

But its spirit is utterly different

Now the day is ending…

It is a time of sleep and silence and waiting

There is a sense of finality about sunset, a feeling of completion

What you have done is fixed forever…

And for aeons old Earth; a damp stone ball has spun on its axis and revolved around the burning sun

And Earth-rhythms have shaped every form of life from amoeba to plant to animal

And they still pulse within us

Still we see the Earth as a huge flat plain, circular with an inverted blue bowl over it

And every day stars and planets rise over the western edge of our world

And we feel stationary while they are moving

But none of this is so

Look to view-point

For what you see is not always true

You are interested in how things appear… and

not how they really exist

Remember that only half the sky can be seen...
half is invisible

And what lies beyond our horizons?

Feelings. secrets and the inner life

And reactions are formed there in darkness...
always hidden from view

One great lesson in spiritual life is that you are
not your body... but a spirit-soul that lives
forever

You were once a child... now you are mature

But where is your childhood body?

It no longer exists, but you are still here,
because you are eternal

The temporary body of flesh has changed... but
you have not

Past times are gone but they glow like embers
in your mind's eye

And that remembrance is like a lamp that
signifies your everlasting life

And the child of the past is still there

You will find him when you laugh and when
you cry

And you cannot act mature until you look deep
within and see that he manipulates you

And tarnishes your relationships

And fills your life with confusion and sorrow

Know that all inner selves must be taken out
into the light before you can know real life…

Then new suns will rise inside you like new
days dawning

And as life moves on

And your levels of consciousness alter upward
or downward

Know that every time you act physically,
mentally or psychically - you have created an
effect that will be returned to you in this
lifetime or a future one

Its echo will follow you

But once its repercussions are absorbed, you
are freed… having paid the price

It will also bring you pain

For the dawning of a higher consciousness will
destroy the only reality you have known

And although self-awareness leads you to
greater freedom and power

Still, as you become more conscious, your
shadow will loom larger than before

And when you step into the light, you may not
see its radiance

But you will be more capable of reflecting it to others

For at first you will see only darkness

Know that only by learning to hold and balance both light and shadow, goodness and evil, will you become integrated

For even as your polarities war violently and sweep you up in a whirlwind of anxiety and tension...

still a new third force will emerge from it all and heal the wounds that split you asunder

Consciously embrace the new energies that flood you

Discover your true self and strengthen it

Take old repressed feelings and needs out into the light

Acknowledge them

Name them and accept them with compassion

Then they can evolve and transform...

And if misery is your shadow

And you find no happiness in yourself

The surest way to contentment is to forget your own personality

And if you tire of people... do not isolate yourself

For if you live in a continual state of isolation of the heart, caring for nothing but your own needs...

You will pass away your life in dreaming of that which you do not possess

And you will lose your substance of spirit and power

And you will become like a vapory dream

For isolation produces starvation

And a desire locked up in the heart feeds on your life if you harbor it

And stored-up anger seeks an object on which to vent itself...

Put aside your attachment to the entity called suffering

Honor yourself and others will honor you

Stop reacting for the needs of society

React for yourself

And you will feel the release of internal chains as they drop away

Rely not on guidance from outside yourself

For although the black smoke of negativity may engulf you at this moment...

know that you will not always be its slave

For the very act of reaching for another state of being

And speaking a word of faith in the unseen will
tilt you away from any dark forces

Let others be responsible for themselves

For they can grow no other way

And when your friend finds his true inner
self… then his feelings cannot be hurt

Only his ego can be bruised

The ego is merely an accumulation of
reflections

For you let others tell you who you are

Cover the mirror and look within

For just as night is swallowed by the dawn…

You are the incarnated result of evolution from
your last life

And your next personality is being evolved
right now in your present days

Passions and vices may die while you live

And if they survive you, they will be born
again

Develop a specific character

For that will live on…

And look not for heaven in the mists of some
future time and place

For it can be here and now…

if you find your true spiritual level and dwell in it

Leave the mental level of tortured thoughts and memories and stiff unyielding attitudes where fear and hostility breed... until your life becomes a hell on earth

Rise from that painful state and bask in the higher realm of spirit where you will be guided by ageless wisdom

For, to be saved is to be saved from yourself and the prolonged agonies of self-delusion and self-betrayal

And the one least able to think for himself will offer to think for you

But his help has a price... and thinking cannot provide a true answer anyway

Take command of your life. Act for yourself by moving up to a higher plane where you will find the truth

Learn to see behind human masks... strive to see people as they really are and escape the pain of deceit

For if you are spiritually alive, no one can exploit you

See through the one who expects you to live up to his expectations

You need give him nothing you do not want to give

Still some will try to hurt you or undermine your confidence by reminding you of past mistakes or shames or losses

And they seek to weaken or confuse you for their own gain

Know that you are not the same person you were one year or one day or even one minute ago

See your real self as renewed every moment and all wounds will heal…

The whole nature of existence is to renew…

Face the death of every moment

Die to things that are over and spent

Let go of the relationship whose course has been run

Or the situation whose colors have all been shown

It is finished

Drop it

You have had the best of it

Let it go

Die to the old self

Slough it off like a serpent shedding its skin

It is a secret of life… to die to things that are no longer beneficial

Die every day in the shadow-chamber of sleep

Then arise reborn

And taste the miracle of regeneration

And look for secret places in your heart

Dare to go there

For the heart is a sacred carrier of profound knowledge

And ancient fires burn within it

Know those heart-fires well

For out of them come the issues of life

And through those flames all things can be beaten like molten metal and forged anew

But know that sometimes a sea of flames is an illusion brought about by reflections of mirrors that should have been covered long ago...

Learn to sort out the threads of your destiny from a tangle of dreams and circumstances

See your life unfolding within a larger awesome pattern

Do not drift, but develop a pliant relationship between your will and the realities surrounding you

Days and years are the blank pages of your life

You may write on them what you will...

For Man's life is a search

And he moves forward without knowing that
the work beyond the horizon is not ambitions
fulfilled or dreams becoming reality

But realization…

And realizations take place invisibly

You contain limitless dimensions

For many past worlds have left their mark in
you as animal, crystal and seed

And you burn mighty fires

Your body may perish into ashes

For reason says you must die

But the flame of intuition is your torch to
eternal life

And so you constantly die

And are constantly reborn

And your past lives are but dead suns whose
rays have left imprints

The elements of the human body are but water
and earth and fire and air

As in blood and flesh and body-heat and breath

And as past lives or present thoughts and
emotions dictate…

So does the body take on many different appearances...

For Man plays his part in one great endless pattern...

As people respond to the earth... the earth responds to them

As Man was born into the world... the world was reborn in him

And there is heat and cold inside you...

As suns rise and moons reflect within... from a solar plexus and a lunar plexus working to keep the body temperature even

One carries solar energy like the sun and the other carries lunar energy like the moon

One is hot and one is cold

The sun cannot be there for twenty-four hours a day...

So the moon must balance by giving only the sun's reflected energy... a cooling effect

So, like day and night,

there are corresponding systems in the human body

And their coming together produces a new energy... like the fusion of fire and water

It is electrical and can be stored inside yourself

Pay attention to these streams

For through lunar energy, an excess of solar energy can be nullified

And these mighty forces should be balanced and made to run evenly…

So, be physically firm, mentally stable and spiritually ready to receive their divine fire

Sunrise and sunset are clear milestones in your day and in your life

For the sun reaches the peak of its daily arc; high noon…

then stops ascending and starts its descent towards the western horizon

But it has yet another milestone to pass; midnight

Then somewhere below the horizon, it stops descending and starts to rise

And the spirit of that sunrise is hopefulness and new beginnings

Still, life-changes do not always occur at day-break… but anytime

The new day is a blank slate

And you may fill it with fear or neurosis or laziness

and make of it what you will…

But dawn marks the inception of a new round of decisions and chapters and chances and possibilities

And there is one great activator, one active ingredient, one unreliable and fragile force: the human will

And the dawn symbolizes that will

For it contains the ability to make choices and intentionally pursue certain experiences...

The sun is the nucleus of your personality

It represents your essence; the inner core of motives and prejudices and desires that shape your life

And the cosmos is a mystery wherein every sound however small

And every thought however feeble, reverberates and is loudly heard everywhere

So that there is no such thing as privacy

And everything is recorded... is never destroyed...

and is always repaid in a befitting manner

And so the endless struggle between Man's ego and his higher self goes on

And he constantly ponders what he should attempt to save...

others... himself... or the world?

But first he must consider the many worlds within himself...

For Man has inherited wisdom of the heart
from his journey through the deep aeons of
time

And you may tap that great stream of insight if
you direct your attention to the physical area
below your heart… the solar plexus

And like the sun from which it takes its name…

it is your great central power-house; reservoir
of the life-force

And like the rays of the sun, its filaments
extend in all directions to nourish the body's
vital organs

Project all your feelings towards this abdominal
brain

For there lies the sacred tabernacle of God's
fire

Breathe into it and swallow its precious flames

Focus on its blinding light

And all obstacles can be overcome… any battle
can be won

For there you will find all the power you will
ever need

Identify your own heart with the great cosmic
heart

And you will feel a spiritual expansion

And you will embrace all the universe that is
and ever will be

For one vast heart carries the source of all light
and life…

See that Man is like the fool in the Tarot card
wandering along…

A vagabond going his own way

And he carries a bag containing universal
knowledge

But he doesn't open it

And he walks towards a precipice

For he can so easily fall into the bondage of
material desires

And the sun, like his spirit, rises behind him

But it never reaches its zenith

For if it does, it will descend and decrease its
power…

Give yourself powerful keys to ponder…

Regeneration

Reincarnation

Revival

Renewal

Resurrection

Surround yourself with the yellow light of sun

For you need not leave your own space to fly

and expand

Reach out and touch the universe

And look down on small troubles… for they
will melt in your heart-fire

For the sun of pure consciousness shines in the
chambers of your heart like a self-luminous
spirit; a sun of suns

It is the inner self that transcends words and
thoughts

And once you realize its presence, you will no
more return to this world of birth and death

And the truth will ring inside you; nobody
comes and nobody goes

The soul exists forever

Burn through your fears and delusions with the
power of enquiry

Have the courage to always climb upwards

Aspire to the higher world

And know that courage itself is power

For you have control over what kind of dance
you do to the solar-music of the sign under
which you were born

It is not all wasted stars and dead suns

For all the patterns are imprinted on your
subconscious mind… trailed from lifetime to

lifetime… ready to be activated in your present existence

For there are stains on every heart

And even your physical body echoes the past and cries for the future

Listen to those crying voices

Heed them well and resolve

For the body has a million eyes and a million mouths that must be fed

And everyone you have ever been is carried within you layer upon layer

Explore yourself

And through yourself… the universe

And if someone's touch does not feel pure

Know that the whole of the person's past is carried in the hand…

Repressed anger and repressed hatred… all are there

Know that you can control human storms by understanding them

Cruel people have no real power

They know it… and when you know it , you will be safe from them

The cruel one is an egotist

Yet he does not believe in himself… neither should you

He has nothing of value to give you

Let him drop from your experience

Please not the vicious for you only encourage their destructive ways

See that you have fantasies about people

For often you see them as you want them to be and not as they really are

Fear not the loss of your wrong ideas about a person

Simply remove him from your world. Free him. Free yourself

See the enormous pressure inside the cruel one as he explodes with thunderous words and blows because he cannot direct his misused energy any other way

You cannot change him… but you can sever the chains that bind you to him

See his pathetic ignorance.

Develop and live in your own secret spirit-world where you will be safe

For you will never think anyone out of your life

But you can direct the penetrating fire of understanding through all problems until they are charred out of existence

Increase your motivation to overcome past patterns and experience wholeness

And build a sense of trust in your true self

Relinquish your victim-stance

Or your self-righteous sense of virtue

Or sympathy from others to which you feel entitled

And enemies outside yourself... on whom you have directed anger or blame

Then take charge of your life. Feel empowered and increase your self-esteem

Create a constructive image of your new self

Visualize the life you can enjoy if you employ more of your inner resources...

Build on your new intention

And as the energy of your desire for change grows... it will eventually become greater than the fear which prevents transformation

Believe that you can change

And that greater fulfillment is what you deserve

And as you regain disowned facets of yourself... you will feel more complete and open to love and pleasure

And the powers you have so long invested in others will become rightfully yours at last

Know that nothing happens without a reason…

For there is a divine logic that permeates existence

See the past, present and future as continuing phases, each arising from the previous one and leading into the next

And you will feel freed from the vice-grip of fate

And you will take control of your destiny

For in seeing the entire process of growth you can channel your energies towards the highest flowering of your potential

Freedom versus love…

Dreams versus reality…

Pleasure versus responsibility…

The battle of everyday life goes on

And so many times your individuality comes out of hiding and takes a stand

And miracles and horrors are endured or overcome or transformed according to your level of being

As, scarred by experience, you learn courage and endurance and compassion; living symbols of identity

For each one of us is a web of contradictions

And we are haunted by memories and swayed

by premonitions and tormented by dreams

You love. You fear. You create.

And to live effectively in the world you have had to build a personality; a role you have to play

And so you wear the required mask; an outer expression of your inner needs

And you internally live out the past

And time and again you play for yourself old dramas and agonise through musty old scripts

And you wallow within the sanctuary of that underwater prison

Then, daring to expand into a new consciousness, you push against the barrier that suffocates you

Until it gives way and you burst forth into new golden life

And as you dare to swim in the light of change

Trust the new birth taking place within you

Fill yourself with the breath of new life and fear will dissipate

Open to the light of self-compassion and be healed by it

Feel your hatred and cruelty, anger and confusion

Bring those dreaded facets forth into your consciousness from the murky subconscious where they have lain for so long

See that your true self has lived in hiding, awaiting birth, while only false images sustained you until now

And sometimes as you shed your illusions

And circumstances force you to let go of past relationships, false identities or roles you have played

You face the cold desolation of mourning what you have lost… without yet knowing what you will gain

Know that new seeds are breaking through old ground even as you doubt

For they have been subliminally planted by your desire to change

And old structures are already breaking down

And the more you reach forward towards new horizons the easier it will be for you to let go of the past

Listen for the subtle birth-sounds of new seeds within you

Water them with your attention

And they will flourish through your encouragement

And you will witness the glorious process of rebirth and recovery of lost dimensions of your inner being

Then honor your multi-faceted personality

Take charge of your life and liberate yourself from self-defeating bonds

For too long you have been shadowed by the persistence of negative memories that spoil your present days and block your path to a higher plane

Work on recovering positive images from your past

And know that the more value you place on your real emerging self, the more you will let go of the false self with which you have identified

And the more fulfillment you will know

For compulsions, addictions and obsessions all stream from the shadowy subconscious... often fighting violently against the conscious will of the man

We all carry imprints from our families, our cultures and our personal experiences

All are stored inside

And how you react to those influences is what shapes your destiny

The lions of yesterday and tomorrow guard
your present

Dive deep and find your patterns

Examine them and decide which incarnation
left them as marks

Then sift them out and choose wisely

What stays, what has brought you joy and what
has brought you pain and what has troubled
you and what has lifted your heart…

Keep the streams of light and discard the
shadows… for they will vanish as light floods
through them

For fear threatens the self-image you have so
carefully molded

And it threatens the sexual role you have
chosen

And you dread shame or loss of control

And in relationships you vacillate between
fears of too much closeness or not enough

And you fear the suffering that others can
inflict: criticism and rejection, humiliation and
invasion

And vulnerable and insecure, you fear the
aggravation of opening old wounds

And the sense of being overwhelmed by facets
of yourself which have been condemned in the

past, even by yourself as well as others

And your greatest fears may be threats to your physical body or to your identity

And so you cling to the familiar parental voices within

Lest you re-experience the traumas of childhood which could plunge you headlong into the black abyss of terror; the world of the frightened, rejected child… abandoned and alone…

And some inner guardian ardently defends the gate that seals off the pain and anxiety of old wounds

When shadows play at the edge of your mind…

Become your shadow-self

Woo the distrustful child out of the darkness and back to life

For shadows tell us what we fear

And draw smudged pictures of dreads we are afraid to feel

Penetrate them

Face them and you will balance your inner self and the persona you present to the outside world: the mask

For within those smoky depths are stored nightmares: the worst images we have of ourselves

Shadows are places of mysterious fears

There is no sun there

And they represent the lowest point; the nadir of our existence where ghastly forms loom and lurk in their dark corners, writhing and draping veils over the light of our days...

For the shadow is the secret arena of the inner self

And no one outside of ourselves can see it

And when we dare to enter therein, we disappear

And all our energies are directed inward towards the dark unconscious

For its locked-up material must be brought into the conscious mind if you are ever to feel complete and whole and at peace

Still, some choose to live in those shadowy worlds where dreams, nightmares and realities are forever confused...

Constantly moving in and out of each other

So decisions are impossible to make

And facts are hopelessly distorted by propaganda or fears

And outward lives reflect the pathetic inner struggle

As the confused one flits around endlessly in pointless circles

From task to task

From opinion to empty opinion

And he chatters on, pouring out streams of words with no substance

Without purpose

Without direction

Without hope

And in encountering your shadow-self, you may wonder how you can live with the discovery of your own ugliness and potential for evil

For you will glimpse terrifying energies within, gaining pleasure from revenge or planning the downfall of those who have hurt you

And you may even uncover a masochistic craving for physical or emotional self-abuse

For discovering inner demons is a terrible blow to your self-esteem

Know that the first experience of bringing those bad energies out is always the worst

But once out of the darkness, they lose power and evaporate in the light

Learn to trust the beauty within, while tolerating your darker side

For it is a paradox that the process of spiritual growth involves lessening your attachment to your ideal images of self and others and embracing instead your lowest, most vile self

And if at first you feel threatened or repulsed by your hidden facets

Know that you can only discover the buried treasure within by being willing to embrace the distrustful, un-cooperative child

Love and understanding will eventually open the lock

See the most evil parts of yourself as the methods of survival for a terrified child whose needs have been distorted by years of emotional neglect and abuse

Seek out the child's needs

Meet those needs and soothe his fears

Confront him, touch him

Tell him you are a friend from his future

And that you understand his pain

And you will never leave him to suffer alone

And you will create for yourself the nurturing conditions that lead to transformation

Then open the channel of healing love and compassion for others

For only then will the twisted, unredeemed

facets of yourself and the evil hiding within, be
countered and melted by warm feelings

Then you will at last feel compassion for
yourself

Know that all energies can be re-channelled
and used for either destruction or construction

You are the director of great powers locked
inside

The expression of them is yours to choose

Unlock your star-patterns

For all stars are within

And all houses can be reached via the human
heart

For the great being called Man should rise on
fire-streams into a future sun, trailing no
shadows of past mistakes

Re-invent yourself

Regenerate and then reincarnate anew

And build a future faith

For you carry your world, for better or worse
inside you

For in each new incarnation, you are the
mountain to be conquered

And you must overcome yourself again and
again

That is the pattern towards a higher thought-world and a better life

So you desired riches and fame and wealth and beauty in this new life

And you were reborn adorned in the raiment of your dreams

But still the state called happiness eludes you

And even the quiet flame of peace cannot be found…

It always hovers just out of reach…

Know that you will be ruled by your affinity

You make your own heaven or hell

Those who love money seek money-power

And thinkers invoke the powers of the intellect

And those who climb socially seek the powers of society

And some seek spiritual power…

Create in yourself the environment to attract the spirit of that which you desire

For anything to be born the right setting must be prepared

Make the milieu…

For when the sun rises, only some buds will blossom… not all

And you cannot blame the sun for that

For as the full moon reflects the sun's light to
the darkened earth in the night

So, no real power is ever eclipsed

For even dark night-hours are endowed with
the power of stars

A flower that has never known the sun and a
flower that has felt its kiss are not the same…

They cannot be

For a blossom that has never known the sunrise
has never known the sun to rise within itself…

It is dead… just a potentiality

It has never known its own spirit

But a flower that has seen the sunrise has also
witnessed awesome splendor…

It has known a deep, stirring innerness…

Create an inner sun of awareness by incoming
and outgoing breath

Move with it

Flow with it

For each morning your sun rises into a new
constellation of stars

Just as new conditions surround you every day
of your many lifetimes

All of life is constantly moving

But one thing remains the same; the burning inner flame… your share of the power called God

And we move around the sun, circling on our good ship Earth…

Yet we feel that we are standing still and it is the sun that is in motion

And we read the sky as a circular symbol of the eternal and the infinite

For Man has always felt the pull of the heavens and looked to it for signs

For are we not children of the stars to which we will some day return?

Douse the dark fires of anxiety, bitterness and pessimism

For no communion is possible with higher thought if those poisonous entities are allowed to dwell

Let the truth-fire penetrate all of your being

And difficulties will melt

And problems will transform into unimportance

Then see for the first time the blinding light of reality like a sun rising inside you

Regret not past behavior

Let go of shame

For the real you is already free if you live in the reality of the present moment

Forgive yourself for past mistakes

For only subconscious forces behaved badly in your name

And you labelled yourself bad

And society called you a misfit

See that label as a wrong identity

Drop it and your true self will fly free

Break the habit of mental replays of the past

And the pain will disappear

For the seeds of past karma cannot germinate if they are roasted in the divine fires of wisdom

And know the flames that teach and mold

See them as disciplines

For one needs the pangs of pain and happiness

Love and pity

Sympathy and tolerance

Patience and compassion

All are teachers

And all come from contact with other souls in various phases and forms

And the fiery mass continually moves...

shaping and reshaping and striving for perfection

For it is the creative work of the power called God

And you are but one small piece in its giant pattern, being burned and moved about from darkness to light and back again… in and out of the shadows

Accept the game and play your part…

Heal your thought of this moment

For manifest in your experience will be the idea that you hold…

Correct it, for all that you are will be its result

Burn away the rubbish

Fan the bright fire of the present

Dwell in harmony and claim it as yours

The past is dead

There is nothing but now

Leave the desert of illusion and enter the chamber of knowledge

For the soul is all light and fire

And its joy is to expand to the universal

And it strives for liberation from personal limitations

Still the anxious ones fear the vital flame lest it take control and they may suffocate

Reach for the ancient fires of wisdom in your heart

Fires of will

Fires of courage

Fires of knowledge

Fires of silence

And you will become your own world

For you will create conditions within

And they will reflect outward like shining beacons

Dwell above the hostility you encounter in the outside world and it will not exist within

And worry not about those who work evil

For eventually their own subconscious minds will react adversely against them…

And when you weary of tormented days and haunted nights

Think not that there is no way out

For you are only seeing human conditions of fear and confusion and petty opinions

Let your inner spirit burn through the worthless material of melancholy and depression

Focus on their opposite fires of love and

friendship and confidence

For fire always rises upwards

You were not born for gloom and sorrow

Rise then on wings of flame

And expand into the state called joy

For it is a fountain of vitality

Then feel your heart widen its horizons

For joy will be a warm glow in your heart

And its magnetism will draw other joyful beings to you

And the cold grip of fear will loosen its hold…

For joy is an essential element in mastering the experience called life

Its power is incalculable

For its warmth will attract beneficial forces just as gloom will attract harm

Know that silent joy is like a fire covered with ashes…

Express it

For its richness can be multiplied by being grateful

Acknowledge it with thankfulness

And it will reverberate through your being and arouse there its own vibration

For to acknowledge something learned or

received is to reflect it within oneself...

And the reflection multiplies its value

Fear not the entity called loss...

lest you attract it

And run not from disagreements with others...

for situations will follow you

Face them and trust in the power of infinite intelligence

For all your demands will be met

And who is there to fear?

A higher power works for you simply because you asked...

Know that only by acknowledging and confronting fears can you overcome them

And only by opening the wounds of the past can you heal them and so discover your strong hidden resources

And only by bearing the anxiety of separation from parental voices within and cancelling out the playing of old rituals can you develop your true self

And only then will you know peace

For only then will you have a true self with which to make peace...

And, afraid of losing yourself in another, you may choose a partner who is incapable of intimacy

Or, afraid of losing the other and being alone with yourself, you choose a mate who needs you so deeply that he offers false security

So, symbiotic and out-of-tune, the partnership endures

For it at least prevents your terror of being alone

But mostly you resist the viewing of the entity called fear

And your muscular body-armor grows rigid against it

For you must keep the fear out of your consciousness

And your emotional life is but a pinched-off stream

For strangely, when you do not feel fear, you do not feel another wide range of feelings and joys and sufferings

And you are less than alive as your meander in meaningless circles, feeling powerless and empty

And if you dare to examine your fear in the light of day

and experience it consciously, define and assess it realistically

Then you can make choices to cancel it or transcend it

For once you are aware of the enemy, you can plan your confrontation, decide your strategy and start your battle

And when you bare your troubled heart to a so-called friend or lover

And you are hurt to see that he is not really listening

Know that he is so worried over his own inner turmoil that he can only pretend to be concerned with yours…

Your only comfort will be in turning to your own voice within

For it will welcome you with understanding and listen to your whole story without condemnation

For your spiritual self will be the voice you hear if you put aside your mental self which worries and frets and tosses you around, changing your identity with every changing thought until you do not know who you are

Stop thinking and relying on the opinions of others and you will rest in the knowledge of your changeless reality within

And when you meet someone unpleasant who wounds you with the sting of insulting words... be not perplexed

Do not allow him to upset you, just relax

Suspend your reaction and turn the problem over to your inner sanctuary whose wisdom will solve what you cannot and give you a measure of peace

See that no enemy can quench the flame inside you

For the only entities really opposing you are within yourself... doubts and fears and resentment, hatred and dark clouds of foreboding

For every bad situation in your life is a thought that crystallized

And stacks of negativity build up, fed by your vain imaginings

Ignite the fire of truth under them

And affirm that there are no bad times in the realm of higher thought

Rout the alien thoughts and words

Starve them out by withdrawing your attention

And faith in the unseen will light your way

Give troubles no power to defeat you

But meet them head-on

Penetrate them with the gaze of brutal honesty

And ask yourself how you attracted the problem in the first place

Then burn it out at the roots with the fire of understanding

Then eat the magic of the power called release

And savor the taste of new words with positive roots

Then fly like a gilded bird into the face of the sun

For you will become an open channel

And universal power will flow through you

And you will be cleansed of worn-out conditions

And freed of tired alliances and threadbare human bonds

Drop all resentment

And free yourself from attachments to negative people

For their warped minds will suck you into their abyss

And you may drown your chances for enlightenment through many lifetimes…

drawn into muddy auras not your own…

held down by hands that know only pain

Break free

Forgive them

Forgive yourself and move on

Move away from them in thought and your
body will follow

Study your far memory

And peer into former lives

Dare to examine faint impressions and flashes
of insight

For the quiet voice of someone you once were
will teach you much… and remind you of
secret chambers once unlocked and lessons
once learned

Befriend all hindrances

And make stepping-stones of obstacles

Let everything work to bring your own toward
you

And walk the royal road

Use your inner eyes and see the tide of destiny
flowing your way

From north and south… east and west…

a bounty of good is yours

The good wind blows your way

Dissolve links with heavy places and bridges to the past

Re-arrange the present

Remove the bad and the good will enter

Expand and receive

And be not afraid to let go

Fear not the loss of everything

For your subconscious mind will call on a higher wisdom

And only the bothersome will be swept away

And that which is truly yours and needed for your sustenance... will stay

For until you are unburdened you will not reach the only temple there is: the temple called freedom

And if you seek something called truth

You are seeking only the truth about yourself

Know that only through repeated incarnations can you attain a lofty goal

For the span of one lifetime is too short

And its limits too narrow to absorb but a fraction of the experience needed by the entity called the soul for its climb towards the white flames of attainment

And problems with others will equal the problems you have with yourself

Do not fear people

But strive to understand them instead

Fear not the arrogant for his arrogance is a cry

Fear not those who insult you

For they are afraid

And when former friends avoid you… could it be that you remind them of their faults?

And if something bothers you… explore your inner depths and examine the real cause

Then decide what it is that really disturbs you, for it may have another root altogether

And know that understanding is on a higher level than merely thinking

For where there is perception… there is no pain

Live within your true identity and you will never be intimidated by another

Then like a naked child on a white horse you will ride into the face of the sun enjoying perfect control between your conscious and unconscious minds

For the sun's rays signify action and vibration

So different from the quiet reflected light of the moon

In nakedness there is nothing to hide

And you will have gained spiritual victory over the lower aspects of your nature…

Know that sun-initiates can accomplish for humanity on the inner plane what the sun accomplishes in giving light and warmth to the earth

And as your levels of learning rise

And you taste new realities

And you make new worlds unique to you and your structure within

Ponder the need for the entity called secrecy

For it will reveal much to you

You have two states of being; inner and outer

And if you show too much of your inner self… you will lose your spiritual riches

They will evaporate in the glare of exposure

For becoming too public is to depend on the opinions of others

But their views are not always the truth

And their judgments may deafen your ears

For your inward journey is private

And in darkness everything is born

As seeds need the dark womb of earth to sprout…

Retreat to that place called darkness to strengthen

Then know the miracle of regeneration

And emerge shining like steel into the layer of experience called the world

And drink the seasons of harvest and rain and drought and storm

Nothing can ever harm you again

For you learned to find your way in the dark

You have been young

You have been old

You have been dead

You have been reborn

And tomorrow you will stand in a place that yesterday your eyes could scarcely see